Robo-

by Sam Gayton
Illustrated by Bill Ledger

OXFORD
UNIVERSITY PRESS

In this story ...

Axel
(Invisiboy)

Axel has the power to turn invisible! This is very useful for sneaking up on baddies. It's also handy when playing hide-and-seek with his friends.

Nisha
(Nimbus)

Jin
(Swoop)

Ben
(Sprint)

Miss Linen
(teacher)

Chapter 1:
The parade

The excitement had been building all week. Axel could feel it: a buzz in the air that made the back of his neck tingle. Now, the day had finally arrived … it was the Lexis City Parade!

    Axel walked through the crowded city with his friends and Miss Linen. The theme for the parade was colour, and the streets had never looked more colourful.

"Look at all the balloons!" said Nisha.

"Look at the floats!" said Jin.

Ben grinned. "Look at the ice-cream wagon!"

"Don't get distracted," Miss Linen reminded them. "Remember our mission. The Head hand-picked the four of you to keep an eye out for trouble."

Axel scanned the crowds. He didn't want any villains to spoil the parade.

"Anyone see anything out of the ordinary?" asked Jin.

"Not me," said Nisha.

Just then, the friends heard a pop and a fizz. They turned to find Ray Ranter standing behind them. He held out a fizzy drink bottle.

"Ranterade, anyone?" he said.

"What are you doing here?" Axel gasped.

The villain smiled thinly. "Anyone can enter the parade, can't they? I've come to advertise my new fizzy carrot juice," he said. "Ranterade ... it's fizztacular!"

"Blurgh," muttered Jin.

"Now," said Ranter, "if you'll excuse me, I need to get back to my float."

Axel watched Ranter walk towards an enormous float. A giant, mechanical bunny-wunny stood on top of it.

"Ranter's here to cause trouble," said Axel. "Why else would he take part in the parade? Everyone knows he hates colourful things."

"We'll have to stay close to him," Nisha pointed out. "Very close."

Miss Linen nodded. "I agree, but remember the rules ... no one must know that you're superheroes."

"We could hide in plain sight," Axel suggested. "Everyone wears fancy dress in the parade. If we wear our superhero costumes, we won't stand out."

Ben grinned. "Great thinking, Axel!"

Axel blushed.

"We'll need a float of our own," Miss Linen said thoughtfully. "I know – we can use the Hero Academy bus!"

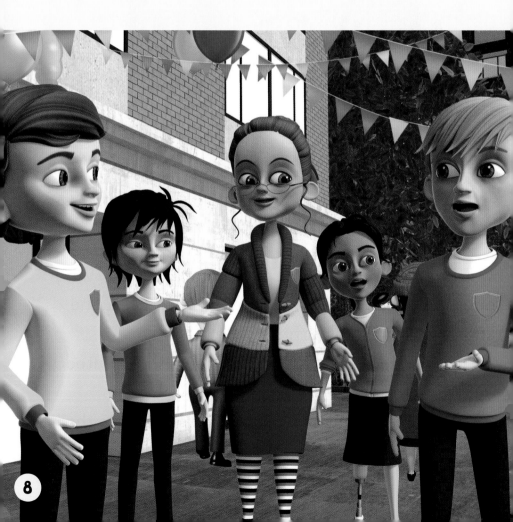

Axel felt his whole body go prickly and hot. He didn't mind *watching* the parade, but being *in* it? He couldn't think of anything worse. "Why did I suggest it?" he thought.

"Are you OK, Axel?" Miss Linen asked.

Axel just blushed again. He didn't want to admit he felt shy about being in the parade.

Miss Linen smiled kindly. "I've got a special job for you," she told him. "One of us should watch from the sidelines in case Ranter's bunny-wunnies are planning any tricks. Could you do that?"

Axel sighed with relief. "Yes, Miss Linen," he said. "Thanks."

Chapter 2:
The Hero Academy float

Axel joined the crowd that had gathered to watch the parade. Meanwhile, Nisha, Jin and Ben climbed on board the bus that was parked down a quiet side street. They spun into their superhero costumes and, seconds later, became Nimbus, Swoop and Sprint.

Using Sprint's super-speed and Swoop's flying skills, the heroes decorated the school bus in no time. Then they got in position behind the Ranterade float, with its enormous bunny-wunny.

The crowd cheered as bands began to play: the parade had begun. All the floats started to move down the street. Ray Ranter walked behind his giant bunny-wunny, using a remote control to make it wave at the crowd.

Suddenly, Axel spotted a horde of Ranter's normal-sized bunny-wunnies hopping towards the Hero Academy bus.

The bunny-wunnies were carrying fistfuls of carrot balloons. Axel was sure they were planning something.

"Miss Linen, watch out!" Axel cried, but the cheering crowd was too loud.

He tried to get to the front of the crowd, but got stuck behind two children in giant strawberry costumes. Before Axel could reach his friends, the bunny-wunnies had tied hundreds of carrot balloons to the heroes' bus.

The crowd gasped as the bus began to rise up into the sky, taking the heroes with it. Axel saw his friends leaning out of the windows. Jin looked like he wanted to fly down to the ground, but he couldn't use his powers with people watching.

Within a minute, the bus had floated away.

Chapter 3:
Rabbit rampage

Ducking into a deserted alleyway, Axel changed into his super suit and became Invisiboy. He knew he was the only one that could stop Ray Ranter, so he turned invisible and crept towards the Ranterade float.

Ranter was muttering to himself as he walked next to the float.

"Perfect!" Invisiboy heard him say. "We're nearly at Capability Way."

"What's he up to?" Invisiboy thought anxiously.

Capability Way was where the secret door to Hero Academy was hidden.

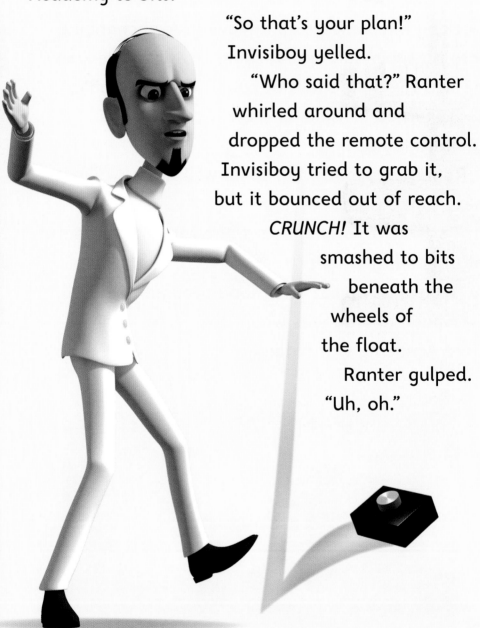

"Time to activate *Robo-hop*," said Ranter.
"My monster bunny-wunny will smash Hero
Academy to bits!"

"So that's your plan!"
Invisiboy yelled.

"Who said that?" Ranter
whirled around and
dropped the remote control.
Invisiboy tried to grab it,
but it bounced out of reach.
CRUNCH! It was
smashed to bits
beneath the
wheels of
the float.

Ranter gulped.
"Uh, oh."

Robo-hop's eye glowed red. Then it jumped off
the float with a massive thud. The ground shook,
and the crowd scattered as the giant bunny-wunny
hopped down the road, crushing everything in
its path. It was a rabbit rampage!

"Stop that bunny-wunny!" Invisiboy shouted,
appearing in front of Ranter.

Ranter's face went as white as his suit. "I can't,"
he stammered. "Not without the remote!"

Suddenly, Robo-hop stopped. It twitched its robotic nose, wiggled its big, metal ears and looked towards Ranter Tower. Ranter had put an enormous carrot on top of his skyscraper, with the words: RANTERADE: It's fizztacular!

"What's it doing?" Ranter whimpered.

"It may be a giant, robotic rabbit," Axel said, "but it's still a rabbit. It's going for the carrot!"

With giant leaps, Robo-hop bounced towards Ranter Tower. The skyscraper rocked as the giant bunny began climbing up to the carrot, breaking windows as it went.

"Noooo!" Ranter shrieked. "That skyscraper cost me a fortune!"

Ranter sank to his knees. His eyes grew as round as a puppy's as he looked up at Invisiboy. "Please help me," he begged.

Invisiboy rolled his eyes. "Fine," he said eventually. "How do I shut it down?"

"There's a red OFF button hidden on Robo-hop's belly," Ranter whimpered. "You just need to get close enough."

There was a screech of twisting metal, as Robo-hop climbed further up the skyscraper.

"Hurry!" shrieked Ranter.

ROBO-HOP

Robo-hop is a super-sized version of Ray Ranter's robotic bunny-wunnies. It took ten weeks to build and is powered by hundreds of litres of carrot juice. Don't challenge it to a game of hopscotch, unless you want to be hop-squashed!

Eye glows red when it is in 'destroy' mode

OFF button

Chapter 4:
OFF button

Invisiboy sprinted towards Ranter Tower. He could hear police sirens wailing, and the giant bunny-wunny crashing away ahead of him. His heart thudded. His mind raced. How was he going to get all the way to the top of the skyscraper? If only he could fly like Swoop or …

"That's it!" he cried, spotting a bunch of carrot balloons tied to a lamp-post.

Invisiboy grabbed hold of the enormous bunch of balloons and started to untie them from the lamp-post. All the while, Robo-hop was getting closer to the top of the tower.

With a final yank, the knot untied, and the balloons rose rapidly into the air ... taking Invisiboy with them.

Invisiboy rose higher and higher. The wind blew him from side to side. He felt dizzy when he looked down. The buildings below sparkled like glitter sprinkled over the city.

Looking up, he could see Robo-hop's metal bottom above him. Then he whooshed past the mechanical rabbit, right to the top of the tower.

RANTERADE:
It's fizztacular!

Invisiboy let go of the balloons one by one to slow himself down. He landed on top of the enormous model carrot. Moments later, there was a grinding crash. Robo-hop was looming over him! It opened its mouth. It was going to gobble up the carrot and Invisiboy too!

Frantically, Invisiboy rushed towards the big, red button on Robo-hop's tummy.

Robo-hop's massive, metal jaws came down towards him. Invisiboy turned invisible and dived out of the way. The jaws snapped shut with a *CLANG* that made Invisiboy's head ring.

He reached for the OFF button. It was now or never.

CLICK! As Invisiboy pressed the button, Robo-hop froze. Its red eye changed back to brown. With a grinding metal noise, it fell from Ranter Tower and crashed to the ground.

Invisiboy peered down at the giant mechanical monster lying on the ground. He let out a sigh of relief.

Chapter 5:
The clean-up

"Well done!" cried a voice, just as Invisiboy made himself visible again.

He looked up to see Miss Linen and the others in the bus in the sky above him. They were popping the balloons one by one, and gently drifting back down towards the ground.

"Come aboard!" Miss Linen said, using her mind power to lift Invisiboy carefully on to the bus.

RANTERADE:
It's fizztacular!

The friends changed out of their super suits.

"What a mess," Ben said, looking down at the city. The streets were full of rubble.

"Don't worry," said Axel, smiling. "I know who's going to tidy it up."

Soon, they were back on the ground. Police Commissioner Jordan was standing beside a sheepish Ray Ranter.

"It was an accident!" whined Ranter. "Robo-hop went wrong!"

Police Commissioner Jordan folded her arms. "Even if it *was* an accident, you can repair all the damage."

"Also," said Axel, "you ought to pay for an even bigger, more colourful parade, too."

"Hurray!" cheered the heroes.

Ranter went pale. "More bright colours? More *fun*?" He looked like he was going to be sick.

"Great idea!" said Police Commissioner Jordan.

Everyone cheered again. Axel blushed, but this time with pride.

The Lexpress

RAY PAYS FOR PARADE DAY

Yesterday, residents of Lexis City enjoyed the biggest, most colourful and fun parade that the city has ever seen. It was the second parade to take place this month. The first Lexis City Parade was ruined when Ray Ranter lost control of his giant robot rabbit.

Local schoolboy, Axel, came up with the idea that Ranter should pay for a second parade, and his teacher, Miss Linen, sewed a fluffy bunny costume for Ray Ranter to wear.

She told The Lexpress, "Since Mr Ranter likes giant bunnies so much, we thought he would like to be one for the day. We called him Ray Rabbit."

Ray Rabbit didn't answer our phone calls, but *hop*-fully he will *squeak* to us soon …